The Cursed Talisman

PYRAMID

THE DESERT

RAIN PUDDLE

THE BURNING DESERT

GO IN

THE GARDEN

VOLCANO

COLORED CRATES

Odd Lands—The Burning Desert
Book two
Copyright © 2020 By Nicole Kaczmarek
All rights reserved.

Text copyright and Illustration/cover art by Nicole Kaczmarek
No part of this publication may be reproduced, stored in a retrieval system, or transmitted, in any form or by any means, (electronic, mechanical, photocopying, recording or otherwise), without prior written permission from the author.
This book is a work of fiction. Names, characters, places, and incidents are either the product of the author's imagination or are used fictitiously, and any resemblance to actual persons, living or dead, business establishments, events or locales is entirely coincidental.
Questions contact, nicolekaczmarek93@gmail.com

Library of Congress Control Number: 2020914750

ISBN: 9798646826597

Art for this book was drawn in the Procreate app

Odd Lands

Book Two

The Burning Desert

Written and Illustrated by

Nicole Kaczmarek

Contents

1. New Discoveries — 9
2. The Burning Desert — 15
3. Something to Smile About — 21
4. City of Colored Crates — 25
5. The Garden — 31
6. Beneath the Sun — 35
7. The Tomb of Wildrew — 45
8. The Talisman — 53
9. Rain — 57
10. Old Friend — 63

7

1

New Discoveries

Todd stood on the beach with the bubbly tide bobbing between his toes. Beneath the bright pink sky, he watched the sun as it slowly sunk into the water.

"Todd! Come on in boy!" Grandpa shouted from the back porch and waved his cane in the air.

After the tip of the sun disappeared into the water Todd raced through the summer wind and hurried inside the house.

"What's up Grandpa?" Todd asked shaking his sandy feet out the door, but Grandpa was already hurrying down the dim hallway.

"Would have told you sooner but it's taken me some time to get this old thing open," Grandpa said overwhelmed with excitement. He scooted his chair over, and there beneath his desk sat a huge hidden chest filled to the brim with old papers.

Todd kneeled and took a handful of the papers, "Maps…" he said in shock.

"And you've been to all of these?" Todd asked shuffling through hundreds of hand drawn places.

"Got that right, all but one…If you want, they're yours," Grandpa said feeling they were in safe hands.

"Really?" Todd pondered the idea of him taking on this kind of legacy that Grandpa had started, but what exactly was it? He never wrote about these creatures in the nature magazines, no one knew about any of it. They were just hidden stories.

"It's all really great, Grandpa, but what's the point of me going to all of these places?" Todd asked.

"What's the point? Boy, it's a life of living! And there's more real treasure out there too. How do you think I got by all these years? But you can't just take it—you still have to help and appreciate those places and creatures out there. Why do ya think I sent you on that first mission, boy?" Grandpa went on.

"I mean, it is an unusually dangerous way to live, and doesn't it get lonely?" Todd said second guessing everything.

"It's only as lonely and as dangerous as you make it boy. The point is to have fun while you're out there in the world—enjoy it," Grandpa told him.

"Hm, I don't know how it'll go but we'll see what happens," Todd said thinking of his time on Oddlen island—a lifetime of those opportunities was in his hands with these maps.

Grandpa peeked at the map Todd rolled up and stuffed in his pants pocket.

"Oh, The Burning Desert…Bring a fan," Grandpa laughed and closed his wooden chest.

Throughout the week Todd studied the desert map and packed his boat with supplies for the trip which would take five days to reach by sea.

Faded notes were written on the back of the map in red ink listing what to bring: a fan, spyglass, bottles of water and lantern.

You would assume there wasn't much to think up about a place you'd never been, but it was just the opposite which caused a few specific questions to pace in Todd's head the night before his departure.

"Hey, Grandpa, did you ever break this curse in the desert?" Todd asked before bed.

"Afraid not," Grandpa replied.

"Well, that's great to know. Why not?" Todd asked.

"That was my last trip before the old leg accident. A partner and I got into a disagreement and well, we went our separate ways without doing what we went there to do. That's why I laughed when out of all those maps you put that one in your pocket," Grandpa explained and limped off whistling.

"I didn't know he used to have a partner," Todd said to himself and turned out the light.

Bright and early the next morning, Todd woke to birds chirping. He popped out of bed, snatched breakfast, and gathered the last of the supplies needed for the trip.

Grandpa met Todd outside near the boat and placed a metal box full of packed lunches on the ledge.

"In case you or something gets hungry," Grandpa said.

"Thanks…This is it then. I don't know when I'll be back, but I'll see you then," Todd said a bit anxious and gave Grandpa a hug goodbye.

"I'll miss you boy—but go on and have an adventure!" Grandpa shouted and hobbled off the beach.

"I'll be waiting…"

Todd started the boat and left for sea, he looked back to see Grandpa sitting on the bench.

2

The Burning Desert

Upon the waves, Todd fished the days away and spent evenings watching the moonlight flicker between the ocean's shadows, and when five days had passed Todd was on the lookout. He searched in every direction for land with his spyglass, but there was nothing in sight, just bright blue sky.

"I follow the coordinates and these islands are never there, I don't get it," Todd said frustrated and headed in the cabin for a snack.

While heading West, Todd ate his sandwich over the ledge and watched the breadcrumbs fall into the water.

"Huh…" he did a double take as a large shadow approached the side of the boat.

As Todd leaned closer a snorkel poked out of the water.

"A scuba diver, how?" Todd wondered and leaned down to snatch the snorkel, but a masked shark popped to the surface and gave a toothy smile.

Freaked out, Todd whipped his sandwich at the shark and watched it disappear into the water. To his surprise, four more sharks surrounded and began to direct the boat with their bodies.

Sailing faster, Todd tried to see through the cloud of fog. He grabbed his spyglass and peered ahead.

"There it is," Todd said, he could see an island cradled by a volcanic rock wall.

The sharks disappeared and let the boat come to a faint drift. Todd was hesitant to drop anchor once he noticed these were shark infested waters, and there was only one entrance through the tunnel way that stemmed from the shore.

Todd went below deck to grab his backpack and looked out the porthole.

"I don't know if a quick swim with hundreds of sharks is smart," he said as a hammerhead zoomed past the window.

He recalled the time Grandpa talked about fighting off five cheetahs with one hand, that when your cornered you'll make do, but Todd wasn't ready for that kind of confrontation.

As Todd came back on deck, bunches of red balloons rose from the water with the snorkeling snapping shark hanging by its strings.

"You're going to need a lift," the shark said and floated away with a smile.

"A lift?" Todd swung his backpack on.

Ding—Ding,

the sound of a ringing bell echoed.

"Ahoy!" said a pink elephant rowing a small wooden boat.

"My name is Rye and I will be your ride."

"Hey Rye—Uh, are you sure your boat is safe?" Todd said as it was half full of water, nearly sunk.

"Yes sir, we're ready to go—hop on in!" said Rye.

"Ok," Todd carefully got into the bobbing rowboat with the elephant, there was little room to move.

"Aye, get back ya beast!" Rye said and smacked one of the black-eyed sharks on the nose with his wooden paddle.

"Get outta here…Here kid, take a paddle and keep 'em off," Rye said as they slowly rowed through the tunnel opening, but Todd was too unsettled to move.

Rye hummed softy as they rowed through the cool violet tinted tunnel where Todd was hit by a smell so salty that he could taste it.

"What's that you're humming?" Todd asked Rye.

"Argh, that's the song of the island; *Oh, I'd wake in the morning and the rain would pour—it'd fill and fill its way up to your door, then the sun would scorch and the water would shrivel, and I'd wait for the rain to pour once more..."* Rye sang.

The whole way through Todd sat silently while Rye whistled and hummed his tune that sounded somewhat familiar.

"Alright, alright—here we are. Thanks for the company. As always, I'll be back to pick you up," Rye said and rowed back down the tunnel humming.

"Thank you!" Todd waved from the black sandy beach.

After a few steps Todd instantly realized why this island was called the burning desert. He felt like ice cream melting in the sun, and the enormous volcano centered on the island gave off an added amount of degrees.

"Whew..."

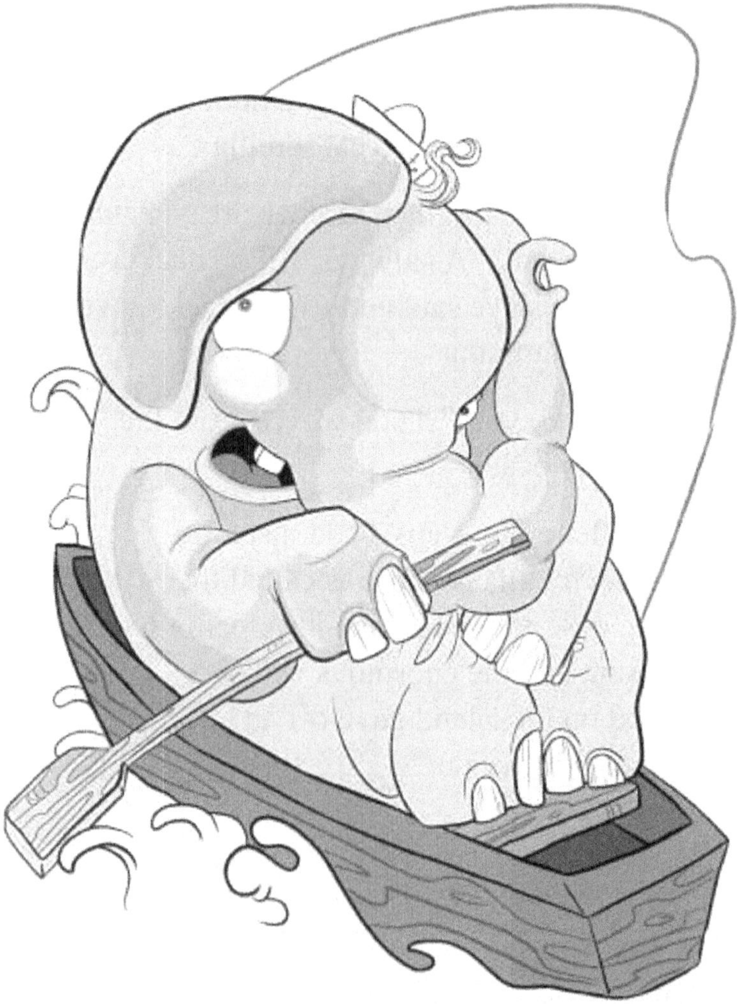

3

Something to Smile About

Todd paused a few meters down the beach after a cloud of sand was thrusted into the air from a small critter dashing his way.

"What is that thing?" Todd squinted and scanned the wide-open beach.

Terrifying little growls grew louder as the critter approached Todd like an open target.

"Go away!" Todd yelled and swung his feet around to keep the vicious fennec fox from gnawing at his ankles, but it wasn't letting up and began to chase after him across the beach.

Todd kept checking back to see the fox right on his tail.

"This thing is relentless, but I shouldn't be scared of such a small little…"

Wham

"Aaahh—who are you?" a blonde-haired girl asked and picked herself up off the ground.

"Todd..." he replied with eyes fixed on the pesky fox jumping into her lap.

"I'm Anastasia and this is Flint. Don't worry he won't bite," she said.

"HA—sure he won't," Todd replied and emptied black sand from his shoe.

"So, what brings you here?" Todd asked eyeing the distinct birthmark on Anastasia's forehead.

"Well, I'm not sure if you've heard of the curse—I'm here to see what it's all about," Anastasia replied.

"I'm actually here to try and break it," Todd clarified.

"What a coincidence, and I see you have a map, is that right?" Anastasia pointed to the old paper in Todd's grip.

"Yeah, why?" Todd asked skeptical of this strange girl.

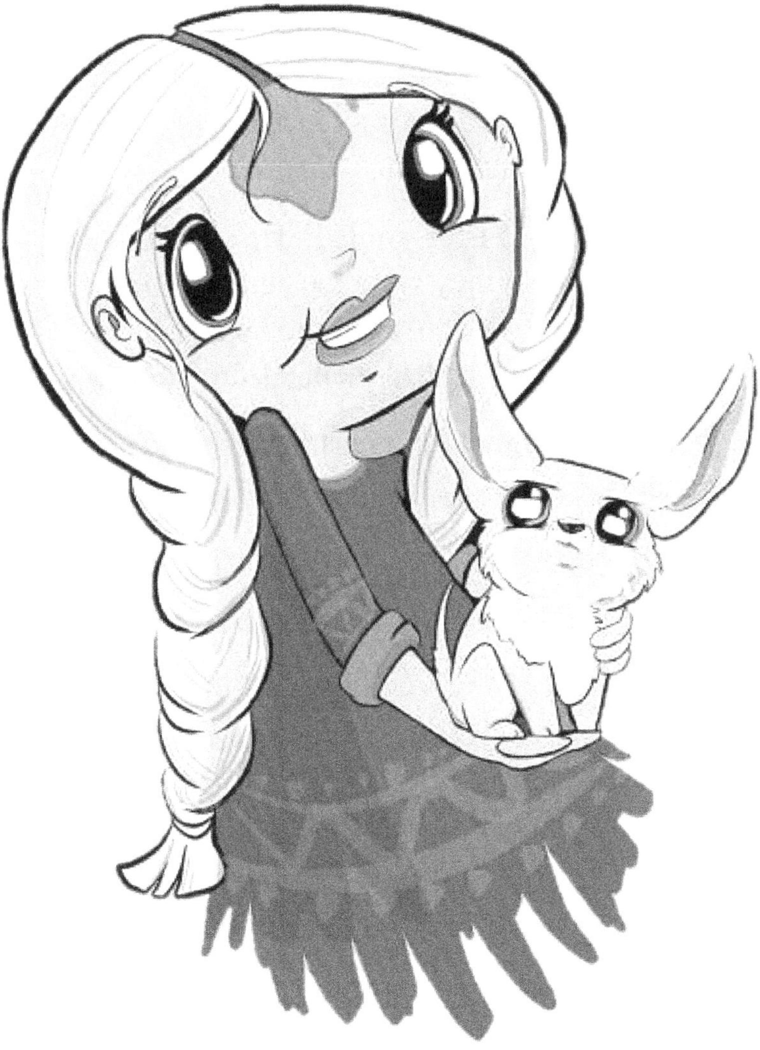

"Cus I've got a book of notes, so if we put our resources together then this should be no problem," Anastasia said and raced off the beach with Flint towards a barren field spotted with piles of hay.

"True…" Todd smiled. He checked his map to find that they were located near the colored crates which was in the opposite direction of the talisman he needed to acquire.

"Guess a detour won't hurt," Todd said and tagged along.

4

City of Colored Crates

Flint jumped through scattered bushels of hay and followed Todd and Anastasia towards a run-down city of green and yellow crates that towered as high as the sky. To Todd they resembled cube like apartment buildings.

"Hello! Is anyone here?" Anastasia shouted, but there was no reply.

The area seemed deserted, but Todd noticed something hiding in one of the ground crates. Carefully approaching he could see some sort of slimy creature, a cross between a frog and badger.

"Come on out, I'm not gonna hurt you," Todd held his hand out, but the big-eyed creature wouldn't budge, it seemed scared.

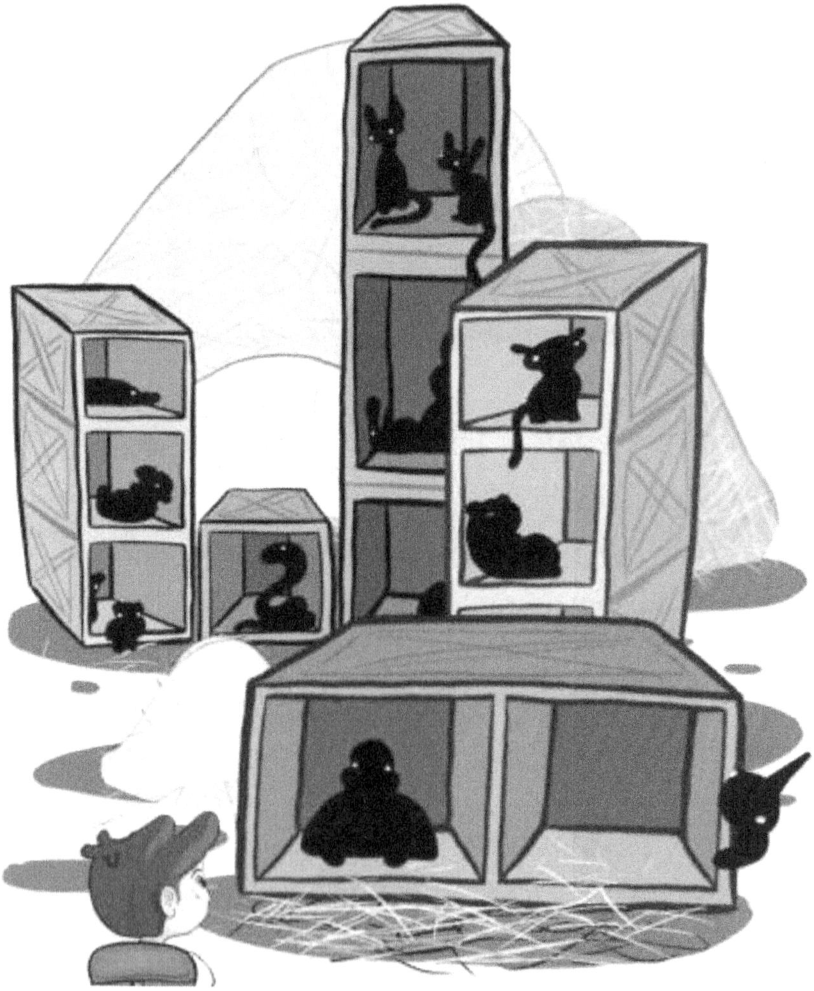

Bzzzzz

"Look out!" Anastasia shouted as a queen bee the size of a car zoomed at Todd with her stinger.

"Woah, wait a minute!" Todd dodged her sharp thrusts.

"Buzz…Why are you invading our village?" the queen bee asked hovering above.

"We're not! We were passing through on our way to the pyramid," Todd told her.

"Pyramid…You'll never find that place, we've searched for years. This is the burning desert, and if you aren't in the shade you will surely fade," the queen bee spoke with arms crossed.

"One by one, creatures have been dropping over the years. We make trips to what's left of the rain puddle but it's hardly enough to keep us alive…Come sit…" the queen said and led them to a dinner table within a large crate.

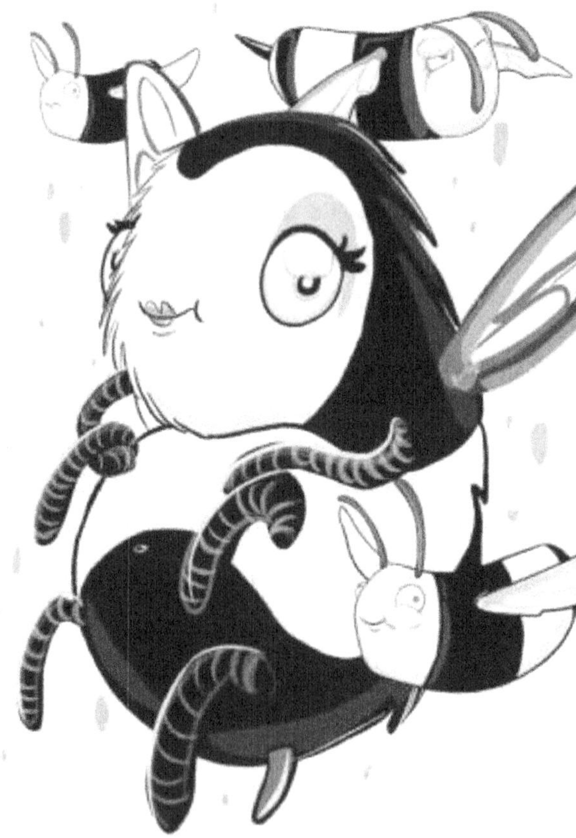

After being seated, four small fluffy bees buttered slices of bread that had toasted in the sun and placed them before Todd, Anastasia, and Flint.

"I came here on a mission to break the curse, and I intend to," Todd confidently told the queen before eating his toast. He in fact had no proof of certainty, but the confidence felt reassuring.

"And what makes us all your mission?" the queen bee buzzed in offense.

"Honestly, adventure, but doing some good along the way never hurts either. Someone's got to help, right?" Todd replied and looked out at all the creatures peering at them from their crates.

"Hm, then we will see about that. If you can find the stolen talisman, the fountain in the garden can be restored and the puddle filled to cool the creatures back into their true homes," the queen said licking butter from her cheek.

"Sounds like a plan," Anastasia said with excitement.

That afternoon, Todd strolled around the crates visiting all the creatures. There were so many different species. It was incredible, but all Todd could think of is what they would all be like at home where they belonged rather in this crammed rickety city.

5

The Garden

Feeling a greater sense of purpose in his heart, Todd waved goodbye to hundreds of creatures as he and Anastasia made way for the desert.

"Come on Flint!" Anastasia called.

Flint ran in circles with the four-eyed baby lizards once more before catching up.

Todd entered a space full of twigs and checked his map.

"We should be in the garden," he said, but the terrain looked nothing like what you'd expect. There were no hints of green, only brown bunches of branches; a reminder of what used to be.

"This entire island is all dried up," Anastasia touched a dead rose and watched as it broke and crumbled.

"Over here—look at this…" Anastasia said ripping vines from an overgrown greenhouse.

Todd ducked beneath a branch and followed her through the bent doorway. It was like a little house lost in time. He instantly noticed the beautiful fountain that was surrounded by a sizable library stretching along the greenhouse walls. Atop the empty fountain was a spherical snoring statue.

"Is this thing the armadillo? It's alive…" Todd said and knocked at the stone shell.

"Must be sleeping," Anastasia said and dusted off a gardening book from the shelf that seemed to be housing a few snakes.

"Hey, do you think this could be where the talisman goes?" Todd traced a hollow space in the fountain that was shaped like a raindrop.

"Yep, that's it," Anastasia jumped down from a tree stump and held up her notebook showing a raindrop looking sketch.

"Where'd you get all those notes if you've never been here?" Todd asked.

"They were my mom's. I never knew her really, so I visit all these weird places to try and see what she saw, you know," Anastasia told him.

"Oh, I know."

"And what about you with your maps, huh?" she asked.

"My Grandpa just wanted me to have them," Todd said shortly.

"It would seem they were on a similar search, just like us," Anastasia laughed.

"Yeah, what are the chances," Todd said wishing he could ask Grandpa about it.

"Well, now that we know where the fountain is let's find that desert," Todd said stepping over a purple garden snake. He looked back at the snoring statue once more before exiting the greenhouse.

6

Beneath the Sun

According to the map, the pyramid sat somewhere in the North West desert and though it would be a treacherous trek Todd and Anastasia pressed on together like an unstoppable force. With full water bottles they left the rocky terrain and embraced sandy hills ahead.

They walked for what felt like hours and placed themselves in the middle of nowhere. Flint hunted the shadows of hawks as they circled from above looking for a meal while Todd struggled to pinpoint their location, it was impossible, and the desert was draining them more and more.

Todd thought of the story Grandpa once told of the hottest summer.

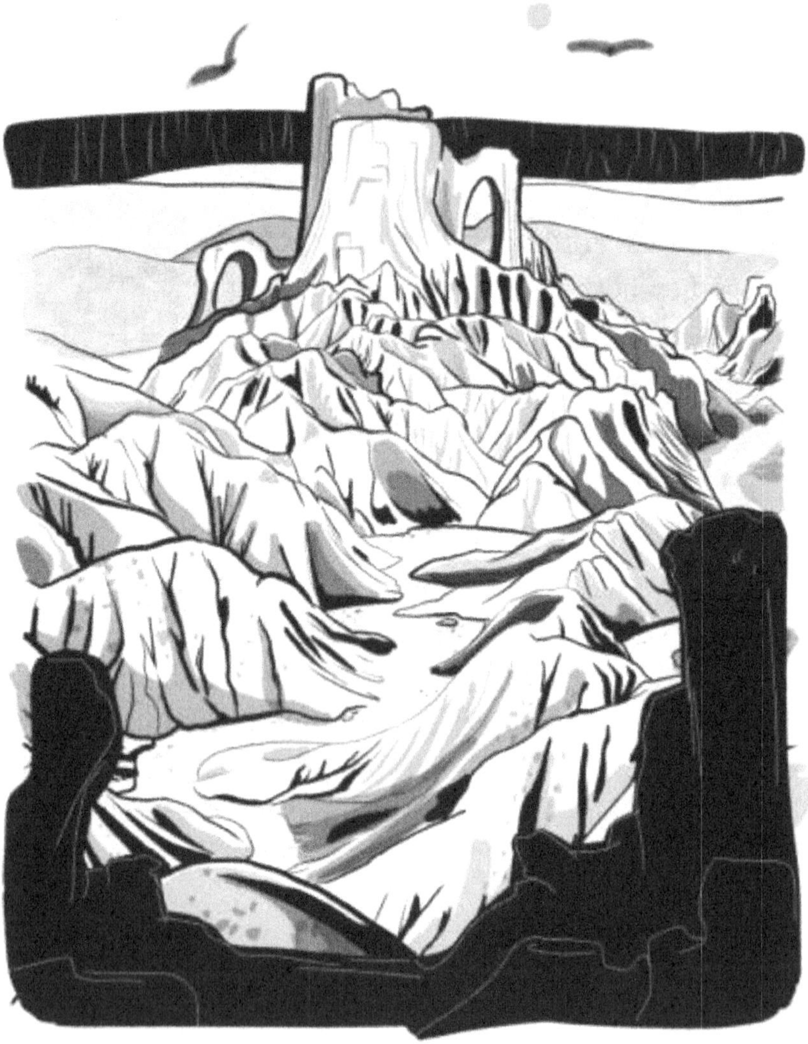

Everyone wore barrels of water like it was a fashion statement, and he had to dig a ten-foot hole in the mud just to stay cool, but Todd was too tired to try any cooling tips at this point. All he wanted was relief.

"Wow, that pool looks great right now," Todd said beginning to hallucinate.

"Nothing like a blue sky of water in the beach," Todd said as streams of sweat rolled down the sides of his reddened face.

He began to skip with glee through imaginary pools of water alongside a stampede of camels. All Anastasia saw was him taking sinking steps into the sizzling sand.

"Please! Slow down and save your energy!" Anastasia gasped with growing concern. There wasn't an ounce of shade out here nor anywhere to rest.

Todd plunked down in his tracks to wait for Anastasia and Flint. He giggled and looked to the blindingly white sky imagining sparkles of snow, but a dark figure appeared to be approaching from above.

A chubby beaked creature wearing a vest gracefully landed before him and waddled over to Todd.

"Sir, you've got to watch for the black cats, ok…" a tiger striped penguin informed.

"What cats?" Todd replied.

"Yeah, the black meowing cats! They'll lead you…See them, follow them, ok," the penguin said peering seriously beneath the brim of his safari hat.

The tiger-penguin held his binoculars to Todd's eyes and a-ways-away he could make out a handful of black cats prancing in a line through the sand.

"Oh, okay, that way," Todd said swaying in a daze.

"Indeed," the penguin chuckled and began digging through Todd's backpack.

"Hey, leave my stuff alone," Todd said seeing double and swatted the dry air.

The penguin remained focused, he found the handheld fan in Todd's backpack and began to fidget with it.

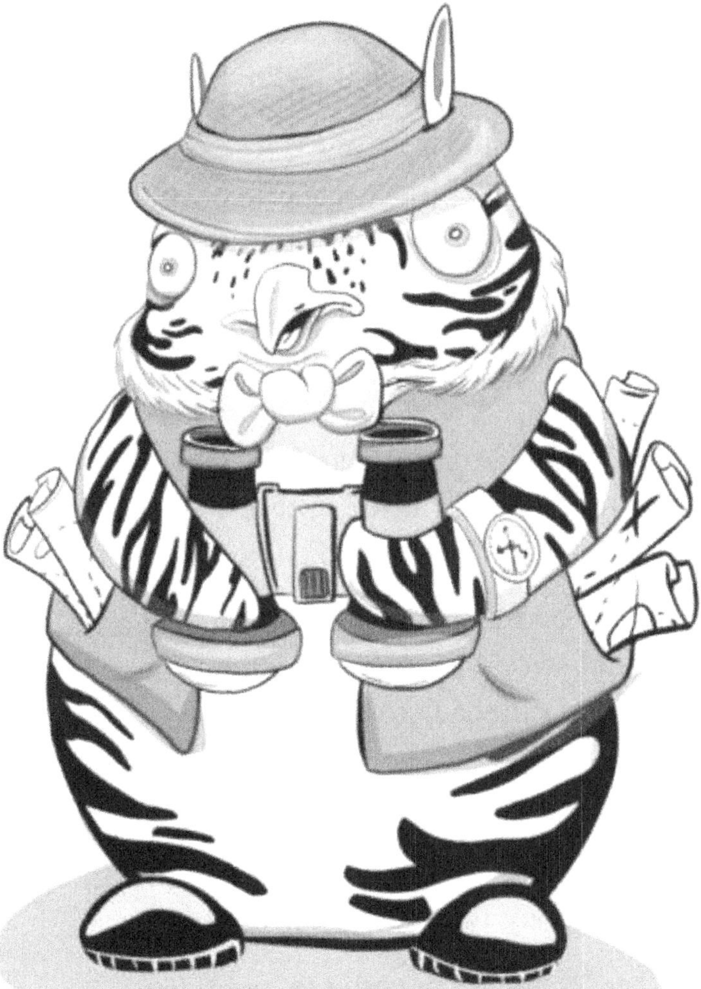

"You don't look so good sir, and a sandstorm is coming—not good," the penguin said placing a bottle of water in Todd's mouth just as Anastasia caught up.

"Who the heck are you? And what about a storm?" Anastasia asked winded.

"You too hold on tight, and remember the cats," the penguin said placing their hands onto the improvised fan. He turned it on and,

Zoom.

Todd, Anastasia and Flint were lifted into the sky and carried away by the fan that acted like a miniature helicopter.

Todd looked back and watched a wall of sand swoop the tiger striped penguin up and send him back to the sky.

"I don't know how much longer I can hang on," Anastasia hollered as she gripped Todd's ankle with one hand and Flint with the other as they flew across the desert.

"Same! I'm going to let go in a second," Todd said eyeing a high point in the sand.

As they passed over Todd dropped and slid down the side of the bowed sand dune.

"Whew…" Todd chugged the last bit of his water and took a minute to regain some strength.

"All this time I haven't seen the pyramid anywhere. How did we miss it?" Anastasia panicked and walked in circles.

"Meow…" a pack of black cats raced passed Todd.

"Cats! That's it!" Todd chased after them with Flint but something protruding from the sand suddenly tripped him.

"What the…" Todd crawled over to a pointed rock sticking out of the sand.

"Come and help me dig this up!" he yelled to Anastasia and began scooping handfuls of sand away from the rock.

The three of them dug and dug until a boarded-up window was revealed just a few feet from the surface.

Flint growled.

"What is this?" Anastasia stuck her fingers beneath the brittle wood to pry it loose.

"It has to be the pyramid, just covered completely by sand…Has to be," Todd said and laughed in relief.

The two of them ripped the board off and a rush of cool damp air rolled out of the open window.

"Well, I'm getting out of this heat," Todd said and crawled into the dark along a slanted wooden plank.

"It's like an attic, but pieces of the floor are missing," Todd yelled back.

"That's a long way down," he said and paused at a drop where the plank was splintered and broken.

Creak

"Hey, not so close Anastasia," Todd said feeling a bump at his foot, but it tapped again, only harder.

"Seriously, watch it there's a drop," Todd said and turned his head to a have a beastly black cat hiss and pounce aggressively onto his head.

    While Todd tried to stop the cat from batting, he slipped. They both were sent off the edge of the plank and down into the darkness.

    "Ahhhhh!"

Poof

    The cat landed on its feet, and luckily Todd had fallen onto a pile of somewhat soft sand. He stared up at the single ray of sunlight while Anastasia wheeled herself down in an old pulley elevator.

    "Are you alright?" she asked.

    "Yeah…" Todd said and picked up his map.

7

The Tomb of Wildrew

"So, we've magically found the pyramid, now we have to locate the hidden talisman in this giant dark place," Anastasia said and lit an old piece of wood to use as a torch.

Using the lantern from his backpack, Todd observed four different passageways. One blocked, one thin, and two placed between Anubis statues.

"Looks like we're on our own again, this map is of no use down here," Todd said with a hand to his face.

He recalled one of Grandpa's stories about the time the sun sunk for fifteen days; in what feels like an eternity of darkness there is always a light even if it does not glow. Grandpa had found a plant that he could eat for temporary night vision. He'd say, there's always a way.

"So, which door? Is there anything in your notes?" Todd asked.

Anastasia flipped through her notebook to a single page of scribbled arrows and symbols.

"My mom wrote a little about the pyramid, but not much. Maybe we should try the doorway beneath the sun symbol and hook three rights," she suggested.

"Ok, I'll go first," Todd said and held out his lantern.

There were cats running and hiding everywhere, parts of the floor had flooded, and clammy cool breezes howled in the halls—it was the exact opposite of the desert above.

"Stop! What is that?" Todd said quietly.

Blindfolded mummies were roaming around the pyramid as well, bumping into walls and grunting. Not wanting to find out whether they were the friendly kind or not Todd and Anastasia shielded their lights with their hands and carefully snuck around the stinky mummies.

Turning at the final right, they entered a large room packed full of treasures. Oil paintings hung on the wall, old rugs covered the floor and knick-knacks were piled all around.

"This is kind of incredible," Anastasia said heading down the stone steps towards a golden scorpion.

"This is it!" she shrieked.

Todd ran over with the lantern and held it to the scorpion, a rainbow glow sparkled from within its claws, it was the raindrop talisman.

"Wooowoooooo-Who's there? Who dares to enter the tomb of Wildrew?" a deep voice echoed in the room.

Anastasia held on to Flint as he began to bark uncontrollably.

A gust of wind blew past, the old torches lining the room lit and revealed a ghostly slithering six-armed panda snake.

"What do you want?" Wildrew the ghost danced towards them.

"We're here to take back the talisman you stole!" Todd shouted.

"I did no such thing, but if that is what you seek then you may have it by answering my riddle," Wildrew said; his snake-like tongue slithered between his teeth.

"It pats at your door and does not rhyme with the number four, in so many shapes it can take so many forms," Wildrew told the riddle in a ghostly giggling tone and waved his arms from side to side.

"That's easy, and that's why we need the talisman…Water!" Todd said without a doubt.

"Uh, well you'll never get it!" Wildrew tried to snatch the talisman from the scorpion's grip, but his ghostly hands could not.

"I order you to leave now, or I will summon my metallic army," Wildrew said drawing in the air with his hands.

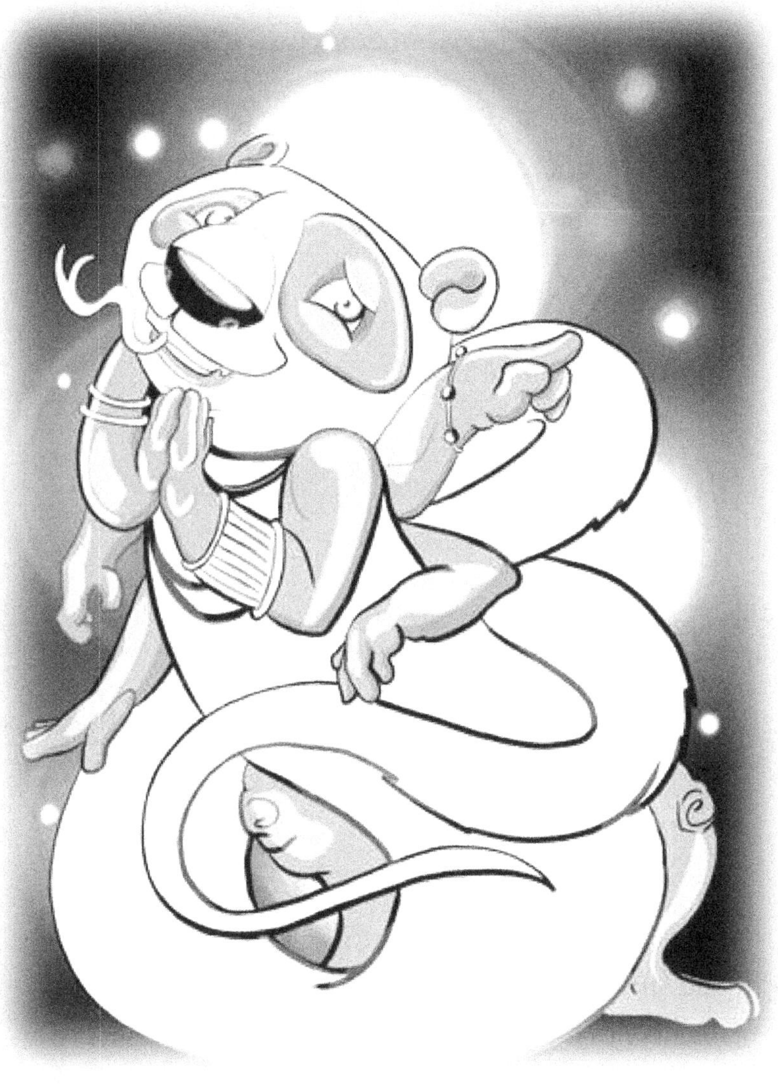

Before Todd and Anastasia could reply metallic colored scarabs poured in from every crevice and gathered in a mass to take the talisman away.

"Flint, no!" Anastasia called out as Flint scampered after Wildrew.

"I never liked rain—it always canceled all my parties," Wildrew said slithering away around the room.

Bark-Bark!

"I think can get the talisman," Anastasia ran to the second-floor balcony.

Bark...Bark!

Flick caught up with Wildrew's ghostly tail and chomped his behind.

"Ahhhh!" Wildrew screamed. He fell backwards into his sarcophagus and burst into teeny specks of light.

Just as Anastasia was to jump from the balcony into the scarabs they began to drop and quickly dispersed. The talisman fell to the floor.

"I've got it," Todd said happy to have it in his hands.

As Anastasia approached Wildrew's sarcophagus, the door to the room began to close. The walls shook, and sand began to sift in from the ceiling.

"Boobytraps! We need to go, now!" Todd said.

He nestled the talisman in his backpack and tugged at Anastasia's hand, but it seemed part of her didn't want to move—her eyes were fixed on something.

Flint began to tug at her shoe.

"I can't leave you here! What are you doing?" Todd shouted as he and Flint tried to drag her along.

The heavy stone door was lowering. If they didn't move now in moments they'd be stuck forever. Racing up the stone steps the three of them ducked and rolled beneath the solid door.

Picking up the pace they continued down the halls, Todd tried to remember the pattern in which they came from but backwards.

"Left, left, ahhh!" Todd screamed as a mummy stumbled out in front of him, they were everywhere. Holding onto Anastasia's hand Todd plowed through the barrier of moaning mummies and blasted out. His lantern was dimming but they were almost to the elevator.

 The boobytraps caused the pyramid floors to shift and form a steep split. Flooding water rose with the temperature and heavy thorny vines swung down like spiky pendulums.

 While dodging falling bricks, they hurried onto the pulley elevator and traveled up as fast as possible. At the last moment the three of them leaped onto the brittle plank and crawled out the window into a plethora back cats that were lounging outside.

8

The Talisman

"I never thought I'd see this sand as safety," Todd said rolling beneath the burning sun once again.

"Yeah, I can't believe we did it," Anastasia said lying beside him.

"Alright, back to the armadillo then?" Anastasia asked ready to go.

"Woah-woah, wait…What happened back there with you? If I hadn't pulled you out of there you may have been stuck forever—that wasn't cool!" Todd said.

"I'm sorry…I saw a ruby in that room. My mom wrote in her notes that she wanted it for something important. I just froze knowing I couldn't get it but didn't want to leave it and let her down," Anastasia explained.

"Well listen, there's all kinds of treasure out there, so don't beat yourself up," Todd assured with a smile.

Flint hopped inside Todd's backpack and scarfed down one of the sandwiches before cuddling up for a nap as they returned across the desert.

"I think he's warming up to you," Anastasia whispered over Flint's small sleepy snores.

"That'll be the day…Hold on. Shh…Do you feel that?" Todd did a three-sixty and checked their surroundings.

"What? What is it?" Anastasia asked struggling to keep her balance as the ground started to rumble. A swarm of something was coming up from behind.

"I don't think I'm imagining things this time—meerkat wave!" Todd shouted.

As they were swept away in a huge herd of rambunctious meerkats Flint woke snapping and growling. He slipped out of the backpack and was bounced all around. Anastasia grabbed a hold of him and floated towards the surface as they were conveyed across the desert.

"The transportation service in the desert is really something," Todd laughed as they bumped along.

Closing in on rocky terrain the meerkats dove into their homey holes and plumped Todd and Anastasia on the ground.

"That was convenient—almost there," Todd said feeling a large sense of relief to be out of that scorching desert.

9

Rain

Returning to the garden, everything was exactly as they'd left it. Todd entered the greenhouse and stood before the snoring fountain. He gently placed the raindrop talisman into the stone gap and witnessed the entire garden come to life before his eyes.

Every bush, flower and blade of grass began to sprout, color bloomed into every nook and cranny and the curled-up armadillo unrolled into a lively jump.

"You've awoken me and done it, ha-ha!" the armadillo said stretching his snout in the air to smell the satiny flowers. Like magic, crystal clear water filled the fountain once again.

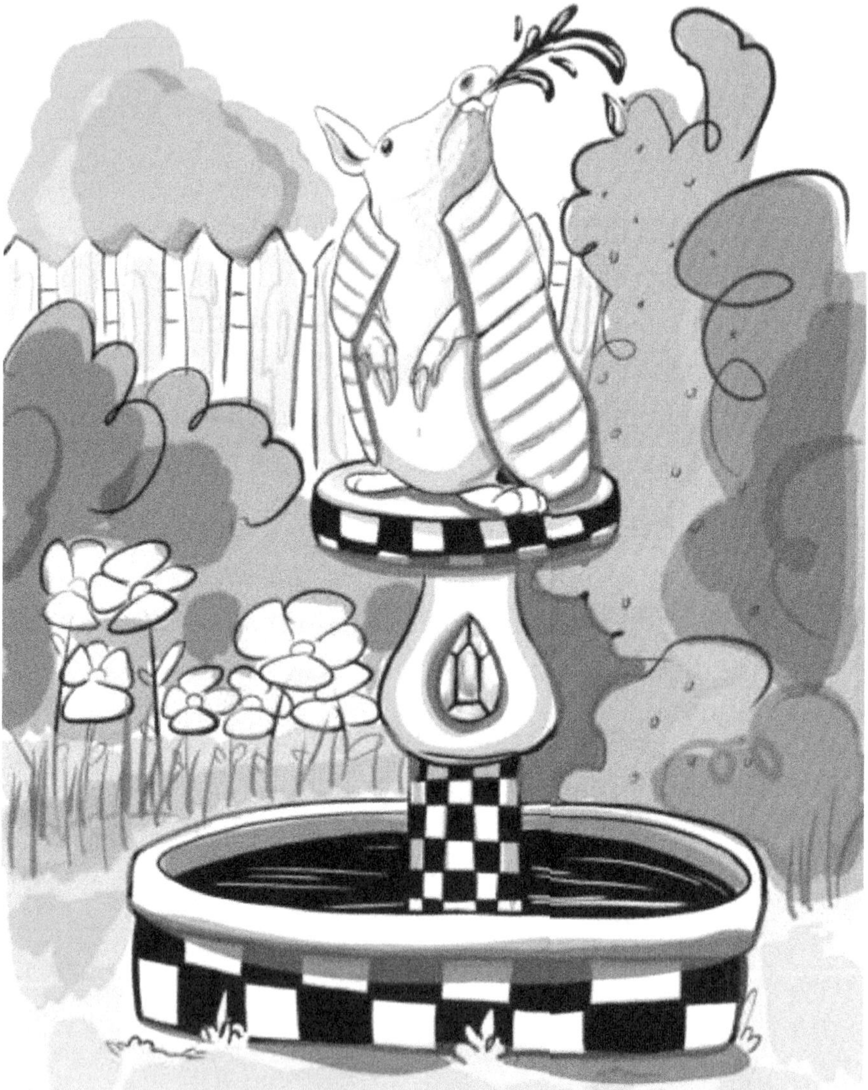

"Wow, all this from a gem?" Anastasia was speechless, she couldn't believe it.

The ears of the armadillo flickered. "I shall sleep no more. The rain is ready, the trenches will fill to rivers, and the puddle will rise," he said and spat a stream of water.

"The great drying is over!" a shelled critter said scurrying by.

"Go…Go out and enjoy the rain! Tell the others!" the armadillo encouraged and began a powerful rain dance.

Grey clouds took over the sky as Todd and Anastasia left the greenhouse. Everything looked completely different, like a whole new island. They passed back through the city of colored crates to see all the stuffed-up creatures moving out in a single file line.

"Where are you all going?" Todd asked.

"Back to the puddle, back home!" said a shaggy white moose.

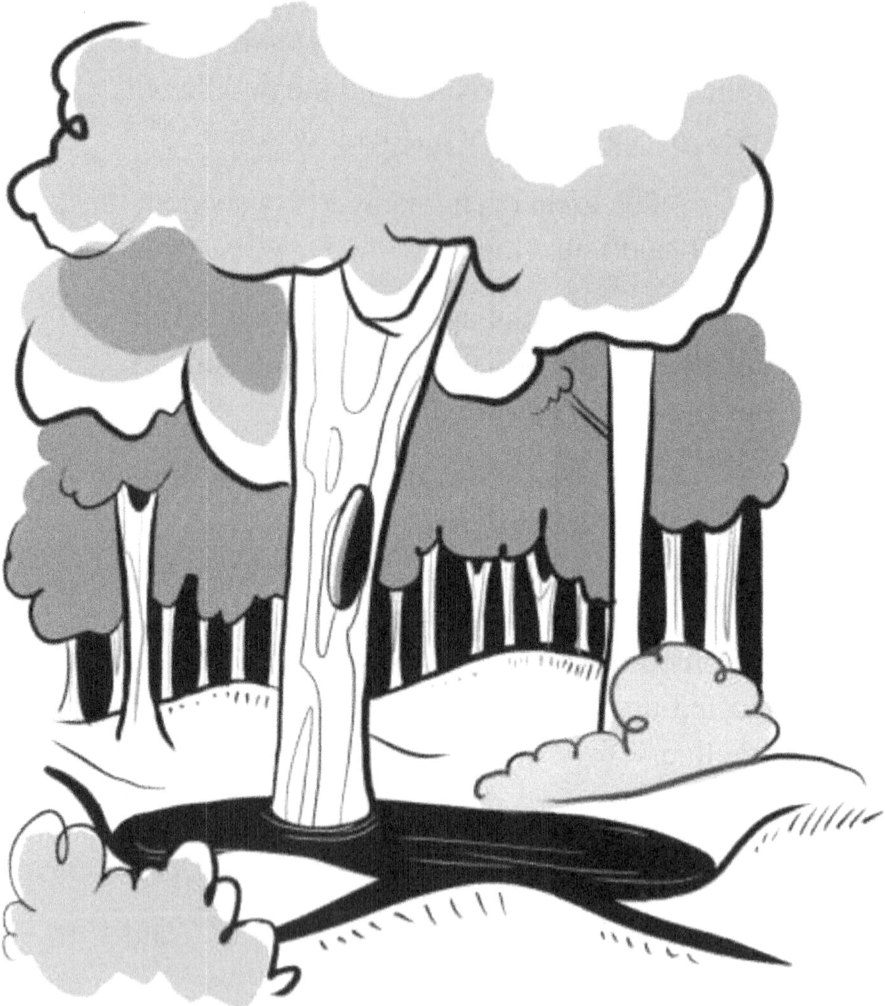

"I never thought I'd see the day," the queen bee buzzed and happily zoomed off towards the flowery garden.

Tiny water drops began to fall, and the rain began to pour like never before. Feeling much cooler, Todd and Anastasia followed the trail of creatures to the rain puddle.

"Everyone's so cheery—well, besides Wildrew but..." Anastasia said watching baby ducks splashing in the growing puddle.

It was a sight to see a home reclaimed, but after such a journey, it was also time to go.

Flashes of lightning and thunder boomed over the volcano. Todd watched a gush of lava spew from the top and burst into fireworks that spelled out,

Thank you.

"So, how are you getting home?" Todd asked Anastasia.

"I kind of parachuted from a plane to land here, so not sure yet," she replied.

"Ahoy, fellow fellows! Knew I'd see ye again," Rye the elephant winked and rowed towards them from the tunnel.

"Where's home for you?" Anastasia asked holding Flint tightly as they squished into Rye's rowboat.

"Winsel, have you heard of it?" Todd asked and noticed Rye humming a different tune than before.

"I don't think so, but for us a home can be found anywhere so—Winsel it is!" Anastasia shouted while Flint persisted on nipping at Rye's trunk.

"Right, here we are back to the ol' boat, you're welcome for the lift anytime as well as you lady!" Rye said and rustled Todd's hair.

"And uh, give that little feller a bone, he's like a shark out of water," Rye pointed to Flint and hummed away rowing.

"Thank you," they replied in sync.

10

Old Friend

Over the five-day trip back home, Todd and Anastasia caught up on some needed sleep and talked a good amount even though Anastasia seemed a bit reserved about her private life.

"Finally, we're here!" Todd said approaching the dock. "You're welcome to stay for dinner," he said and hopped off the boat.

"That'd be nice, thanks," Anastasia replied and placed Flint on her shoulder.

In the kitchen, Todd opened a bag of chips just as Grandpa walked in.

"Back already!" Grandpa said, but the smile weakened from his face when he spotted Anastasia at the kitchen table.

"Hey Grandpa! This is—"

"Anastasia…" Grandpa answered after spotting the birthmark on her forehead that sat above familiar blue eyes.

"You know each other, how?" Todd asked perplexed.

"Yeah, how?" Anastasia asked equally confused.

"Your mother Jen and I traveled a lot together, and even at six months old she always had you with her…You came until she went," Grandpa said taking a seat across from Anastasia.

"That explains a lot, like why my notes match your map then," Anastasia said flipping through the worn pages that felt to her like puzzle pieces.

Flint jumped onto the table and went for the bag of chips.

"Well then, I guess we all have a lot to talk about," Todd said and took a seat as well.

Look out for other Odd Land books!

Book one: An Adventure to Remember

Book two: The Burning Desert

Book three: The Depths

Book four: Above the Clouds

(Coming soon!)

Book five: A Sweet Getaway

Made in the USA
Columbia, SC
12 February 2021